In
1935 if you wanted to
read a good book, you needed
either a lot of money or a library card.
Cheap paperbacks were available, but their
poor production generally mirrored the quality
between the covers. One weekend that year,
Allen Lane, Managing Director of The Bodley Head,
having spent the weekend visiting Agatha Christie,
found himself on a platform at Exeter station trying to
find something to read for his journey back to London.
He was appalled by the quality of the material he had to
choose from. Everything that Allen Lane achieved from that
day until his death in 1970 was based on a passionate belief
in the existence of 'a vast reading public for *intelligent*
books at a low price'. The result of his momentous vision
was the birth not only of Penguin, but of the 'paperback
revolution'. Quality writing became available for the price of
a packet of cigarettes, literature became a mass medium
for the first time, a nation of book-borrowers became a
nation of book-buyers – and the very concept of book
publishing was changed for ever. Those founding
principles – of quality and value, with an overarching
belief in the fundamental importance of reading –
have guided everything the company has
done since 1935. Sir Allen Lane's
pioneering spirit is still very much alive
at Penguin in 2005. Here's to
the next 70 years!

MORE THAN A BUSINESS

'We decided it was time to end the almost customary half-hearted manner in which cheap editions were produced – as though the only people who could possibly want cheap editions must belong to a lower order of intelligence. We, however, believed in the existence in this country of a vast reading public for intelligent books at a low price, and staked everything on it'
Sir Allen Lane, 1902–1970

'The Penguin Books are splendid value for sixpence, so splendid that if other publishers had any sense they would combine against them and suppress them'
George Orwell

'More than a business … a national cultural asset'
Guardian

'When you look at the whole Penguin achievement you know that it constitutes, in action, one of the more democratic successes of our recent social history'
Richard Hoggart

Ali Smith's Supersonic 70s

ALI SMITH

PENGUIN BOOKS

PENGUIN BOOKS

Published by the Penguin Group
Penguin Books Ltd, 80 Strand, London WC2R ORL, England
Penguin Group (USA) Inc., 375 Hudson Street, New York, New York 10014, USA
Penguin Group (Canada), 10 Alcorn Avenue, Toronto, Ontario, Canada M4V 3B2
(a division of Pearson Penguin Canada Inc.)
Penguin Ireland, 25 St Stephen's Green, Dublin 2, Ireland
(a division of Penguin Books Ltd)
Penguin Group (Australia), 250 Camberwell Road, Camberwell, Victoria 3124,
Australia (a division of Pearson Australia Group Pty Ltd)
Penguin Books India Pvt Ltd, 11 Community Centre,
Panchsheel Park, New Delhi – 110 017, India
Penguin Group (NZ), cnr Airborne and Rosedale Roads, Albany,
Auckland 1310, New Zealand (a division of Pearson New Zealand Ltd)
Penguin Books (South Africa) (Pty) Ltd, 24 Sturdee Avenue,
Rosebank 2196, South Africa

Penguin Books Ltd, Registered Offices: 80 Strand, London WC2R ORL, England

www.penguin.com

Free Love first published by Virago Press 1995
Like first published by Virago Press 1997
Other Stories and Other Stories first published by Granta Books 1999
Published in Penguin Books 2004
The Whole Story and Other Stories first published by Hamish Hamilton 2003
The Accidental first published by Hamish Hamilton 2005
These extracts published as a Pocket Penguin 2005

1

Copyright © Ali Smith, 1995, 1997, 1999, 2003, 2005
All rights reserved

The moral right of the author has been asserted

'Trachtenbauer' was first commissioned by Writing North for their
Chekhov–Carver Festival, October 2004. Its first nine words comprise
a fragment from Chekhov's notebooks.

Set in 11/13pt Monotype Dante
Typeset by Palimpsest Book Production Limited, Polmont, Stirlingshire
Printed in England by Clays Ltd, St Ives plc

Contents

Penguin would like to extend a special thank you to Virago for kind permission to reprint the extracts from *Like* and *Free Love*.

Extract from Like

What were we like? All innocence, all sweetness and lit anarchy. The slightest passing look or touch flaring between us like a struck match, the promise of something bigger, maybe big enough to torch the whole town. What a time. We've only just begun, don't you remember you told me you loved me baby, the Carpenters layered into soaring harmonies, and the jangling harmonies of those Abba hits and A-A-Afternoon Delight, fracturing without warning into X-Ray Specs and black-eyed Siouxsie, the Jam and the Damned, into being sixteen, seventeen, sharp knowing for the first time. All innocence, raw energy, practised irony, all of us. Catherine MacKenzie brought her Carpenters tape to school to prove that Karen Carpenter was singing 'the best love songs are written with a broken a-arm'.

The world with love

On a day when it looks like rain and you're wandering between stations in a city you don't know very well, you meet a woman in the street whom you haven't seen for fifteen years, not since you were at school. She has three children with her, one of them is even quite old, nearly the age you were when you were both friends, a girl who looks so like her mother did then that you shake your heads at each other and laugh. You tell each other how well you both look, she asks you about your job, you ask her about her children, she tells you she's just bought a sweatshirt with the name of the city on it for her daughter (they're visiting for the day) but she's refusing to wear it and it cost nearly twenty pounds. Her daughter, thin and determined-looking, glares at you as if daring you to make any comment at all. She reminds you so much of the girl you knew that your head fills with the time she smashed someone's guitar by throwing it out of the art room window, and you remember she had a dog called Rex. You decide not to mention the guitar and ask after the dog instead. He died ten years ago, she tells you. Then neither of you is quite sure what to say next. You're about to say good-bye when she says to you out of the blue, God Sam, do you remember that time the Ark went mad?

For a moment you don't know what she's talking

about and you picture the animals baying and barking, snarling at each other and at the different species round them, at fat Noah and his family trying to keep the noise down. Then it comes, of course it comes, God yes, you say, what a day, eh? and as you're walking along the road, late for your appointment, it all comes, it all comes flooding back.

The French teacher, the Ark everybody called her because her name was Mrs Flood. She liked you, she liked you especially, you were clever. She liked you so much that you hated her class, you hated it when she asked you, and she always did with that tone in her voice that meant, you won't disappoint me, you'll give me the answer, you'll know what it means, you'll know how to say it. The day she called you Sam instead of your full name in front of all your friends, like she was your friend or something, you were mortified, how dare she. How dare she single you out, how dare she make you seem clever in front of everybody, eventually you began to slip a few wrong answers in, and when you did the other girls had no excuse to give you a hard time afterwards.

Mrs Flood always talking about the beauty of French literature with her singsongy highland island voice, scared of the tough mainland boys and the tough mainland girls, scared of your class even though you were the top stream, not much older than you herself really, her hair rolled up round her ears like the princess in Star Wars, her eyes like a shy rabbit, her plastic bangles on her wrist jangling into each other as she wrote beautiful French across the board in round letters, *Echo, parlant quant bruit on maine, Dessus rivière ou sus estan, Qui beauté eut trop plus qu'humaine*, pointing to the verbs with the pointer, *j'aurais voulu pleurer* she wrote, *mais je sentais mon coeur plus aride que le désert*, Sam, can you tell me the names for the tenses? she pleaded, and Sally Stewart's friend Donna poked you in the back and jeered in your ear, so it's *Sam* now is it, it's *Sam* now.

Do you remember the time the Ark went mad? The day you came into the classroom and sat down and got your books out as usual and she was standing at the window, staring out over the playing-fields, ignoring the noise level rising behind her as minute after minute passed, ten, fifteen, and each of you realizing that it was as if she didn't even know you were there, she wasn't going to turn round, there wasn't going to be any French today. This was the day that one of the boys had brought in a ball of string and the people in the back rows began to tie all the desks at the back together, a network of string woven between the passageways. Somebody coughed out loud, then someone else made a rude noise and you all laughed in relief, but the Ark didn't move, didn't seem to hear. Then Sally Stewart crept out front and stood there like the teacher, you were all giggling, snorting with laughter, and still the Ark didn't turn round and Sally got braver and braver, touching, moving things around on the teacher's table.

She opened the big black dictionary in the middle, letting the cover hit the table with a crash. The Ark didn't look round, she didn't move, not even then, and Sally Stewart was flicking through it and then she was writing on the board the words *le pénis*, then *le testicule*,

5

les organes génitaux, she got bolder, and in a teacher voice she said, I'm taking the class today since Mrs Flood isn't here. Who knows the word for to have it off? Who knows the word for french letters?

The boys were roaring, whistling, shouting, the girls were hissing high-pitched laughs, someone, you can't remember who, pulled the poster of the Eiffel Tower off the wall and it got passed round the class. You were laughing and laughing in that scared way and then you noticed that the new girl Laura Watt in front of you three along wasn't laughing, not at all, she was watching, her eyes were going back and fore from Sally at the board to the woman at the window, the Ark, the shoulder-blades in her cardigan, her hands resting on the window-sill and her eyes watching a seagull gliding from the roof of the huts to the field. Laura Watt, the new girl, watching it all from behind her dark straight fringe, her chin on her hand, leaning on her elbow watching it. The girl who even though you hardly knew her had heard you say you liked a song and had made you a tape of the whole album, Kate Bush, *The Kick Inside*, and copied out all the songwords off the back of the sleeve for you in her nice handwriting, even though you hardly knew her, had hardly spoken to her. The paper with the words on it folded inside the tape box smelt strange, different, of what it must be like to be in her house or maybe her room, it was a scent you didn't want to lose so you found you were only letting yourself fold the pages open when you really needed to know what the songwords were.

Then Mrs Flood turned round and everything went

quiet. Sally Stewart froze at the table with her hand on the dictionary, it was Sally Stewart who looked scared now, not Mrs Flood, who was laughing in a croaky way at the words on the board and who came across, cuffed Sally quite gently on the back of the head and gave her a push back to her seat.

Mrs Flood rolled the blackboard up and she read again what Sally had written on it. She added some accents to some e's, she put a chalk line through *les lettres françaises* and wrote above, the word *préservatif*. Then she pushed the board right up and wrote in large letters, bangles jangling in the silence, the words Look Upon The World With Love. Then she sat down at the table.

Write that down, she said, write it all down. Heads bent, you wrote it in your jotters, the words look upon the world with love, then you looked around at each other, and you carried on writing down the words on the board, the sex words Sally had found in the dictionary. You were writing until all of a sudden the Ark slammed the dictionary shut and said firmly, now, get out. Go on, she said when nobody moved, go on, off you go, get out, and slowly, unsurely, you all packed your books up and went, the people at the back had to pick their way through the webs of string tied between the desks, and it wasn't until you were out in the corridor that you opened your eyes wide at your friends around you and you all made faces at each other as if to say God! and it wasn't until you were on the turn of the stairs that you let yourself say out loud God! what was all that about? and laughter broke out, and the whole class was clattering madly down the stairs, so noisy that the secretary came out of the headmaster's office to see what was happening and the class was rounded up and made to sit on the floor in the hall until it was time for the next period, and several of your friends were personally interviewed about it by the headmaster though you weren't. Mrs Flood was off school for three months and when she came back you didn't have her any more though you always smiled hello at her in the corridor even though she was obviously a weirdo. And remembering it all like this you can't help but remember what you had really forgotten, dark Laura Watt, and how once you even followed her home from school, keeping at a safe invisible distance on your racer, you watched her come to a house and go up a path and look in her pockets for a key and open the door and shut it behind her, you stood outside her house behind a hedge across the road for half an hour then you cycled home again, your heart in your throat.

Laura Watt, you had found you were thinking about her a lot. You scared yourself with how much you were thinking about her, and with how you were thinking about her. You thought of her with words that gave you an unnameable feeling at the bottom of your spine and deep in your guts. Because you couldn't even say them to yourself, you wrote lists of them in a notebook and you kept the notebook inside the Cluedo box under your bed. In case anyone were to find it you wrote the words FRENCH VOCABULARY on the cover and you filled it with words for the hands, the arms, the shoulders, the neck, the mouth. Words for the lips, the tongue, the fingers, the eyes, the eyes brown, the hair dark, the horse dark (a joke). Words you could only imagine, words like caresses, *les cuisses*. That word was enough to thrill you for three whole days, staring into space over your supper, your mother irritated, asking you what was the matter with you, you saying angrily, there is nothing at all the matter with me, your father and mother exchanging glances and being especially nice to you all that evening.

At night when everybody else was asleep you went through your pocket dictionary page by page from a to z and wrote in your notebook every word that might be relevant. *L'amie, l'amour, l'anarchie, l'anatomie, l'ange, être aux anges, anticiper.* Your French marks went up even higher, the new teacher, a nice Glaswegian girl who looked a bit like Nana Mouskouri, told you on the quiet (she understood these things) that you were the only person in the class who knew how to use the subjunctive. If it were to happen, she wrote on the board. You all copied it down, you watched the heads bent, the head bent three along and in front, you all copied down the words. If I were to say. If you were to see.

In the end you got the highest mark in the class and the only A for the exam in the whole school, you got the fifth year prize and you chose a copy of D. H. Lawrence's *The Virgin and the Gypsy* because it had naked people on the front and you and your friends thought it would be funny to see the Provost's face when he had to present you with it on prizegiving night. But on the night of the ceremony the Provost was a bit drunk, he mixed up the pages of his speech and he muddled the order of the prizes, when it was your turn to go up on stage with everybody clapping he gave you a book called *Sailing Small Yachts* and afterwards you had to go round like everybody else trying to find the right book and the owner of the book you'd been given.

Laura Watt was playing the violin at the prizegiving, she was top in music and was going to study it at university. One of the music teachers accompanied her on the piano and she played something by Mozart, you couldn't believe the quickness and slyness of her fingers on the strings and the way the music went through you like electricity, she was really good, everybody clapped, you clapped as loud as you could, you wanted to tell her afterwards, that was really great, you went up to her and she showed you the book the Provost had given her, it was *The Observer Book of Tropical Fish*. I don't have any tropical fish, she said, I chose an Agatha Christie novel. You both laughed, and you said to her, well done anyway, she was smiling, she said, well done yourself, you're awfully good at French, aren't you? You looked away to the side, shy and caught, you wanted to laugh or something, you said, yes, I am, I think.

Remember that, then, as you stop now, laughing into your hands in the rain, leaning against the wall of a grey office building in this beautiful city. Look around you in wonder again at where you are, remember the first night years ago when you went out with your prize book under your arm and her music still burning in your body, and all the walk home you saw the trees and how their branches met their leaves, the grass edging the pavement beneath your feet, the shabby lamp-posts reaching from the ground into the early night sky; you stopped and sat down where you were on the kerb between two parked cars, you knew the wheels, the smell of the oil, the drain full of litter next to you, the pitted surface of the road and the sky spread above you with its drifting cloud, and the words for every single thing you could sense around you in the world flashed through your head in another tongue, their undersides glinting like quicksilver.

The theme is power

The thing is, I really need you with me in this story. But you're not home. You won't be home for hours yet.

I stand about in the kitchen for a while, not knowing what to do about it, because the story is right at the front of my head, and I decide to do something, I decide to do the dishes. They need to be done anyway (three days' worth) and what's more, with my back to the table standing at the sink I can imagine you, sitting up on it with your legs swinging, eating an apple. So. Listen to this. This is what happened.

It starts with Jackie and I standing at a bus stop in Trafalgar Square. (So it happened quite long ago? you say behind me.) We had taken our rucksacks off; she was sitting on hers and I was leaning on mine, and we were tired and happy, nearly home from a little travelling, still excited by being in such a famous square in such a big city even if we were only there for the half hour it would take to catch a bus.

A woman came over. She was wearing a headscarf tied tightly round her head. This was strange because it wasn't raining, it was mild and clear though it was dark, an evening in late September just after nine o'clock.

Her mouth was a straight set line in her face. Hello girls, she said.

Hello, we said.

Have you just arrived in London? she said.

We told her we'd just got back from Paris, we'd gone there on a Magic Bus special fare of only £7.00 return and now we were catching the nine-thirty bus on our way to stay with my sister who lived with her four sons and her husband near Reading before we went up home tomorrow to Scotland. That was where we were from, Scotland, and not just Scotland but right up in the north of Scotland. We told her all this, detail after detail, without being asked. When one of us had told her one detail, the other would come in with something else. We were charming. We'd have told her anything. I think we must have felt privileged that a stranger had chosen us to speak to out of all the millions of people in London. But more: she'd looked unhappy, and that was a shame.

It's very late to be travelling, she said. You must be tired, coming all that way. Wouldn't you rather stay here in London for the night? I have a flat you could stay in, just for tonight. It's free, you wouldn't have to pay, since it's only for one night. You look like nice girls. My flat is right above Miss Selfridge. That's right in the middle of Oxford Street.

I nodded. I knew where Miss Selfridge was, because I had been to London before on a weekend break with my parents and our hotel had been just off Oxford Street, a moment round the corner from the Miss Selfridge shop.

You see, the woman said, interrupting me. You could go shopping in Oxford Street tomorrow morning if you want, and then you could catch the bus to your sister's.

It's a very nice flat. There's plenty of room, it's very roomy, and I live there by myself.

We both said what a good place that must be to have a flat.

Yes, she said. I've got a stereo, and hundreds of records. Lots of the latest ones, practically everything that's in the charts. I could give you a lift. My car's just over there.

We thanked her very much and I said that my sister was expecting us and would already have made us something to eat.

Are you sure? she said. My car's just round the corner. Or maybe I could give you a lift to your sister's house. Sometimes the buses don't stop at this stop, you know. Sometimes they miss it out on their way round London, and I'm not busy tonight. You're in luck. I could give you a lift.

Some more people came to wait at the stop. The woman stepped back. We thought she must be very shy. We said goodbye and thanks, and watched her cross the road.

That was kind of her, I said to Jackie.

Yes it was, Jackie said. It was nice of her to offer.

I tell you. We stood there, seeing and hearing nothing, myself and Jackie, my best friend, my first true love, below a rumbling rockfall, an avalanche that would have buried us, swallowed us stonily up. We must have looked about fourteen or fifteen to that woman, small and adolescent-thin. We must have looked like we'd run away from somewhere. Naive, bedraggled, in unwashed clothes after a week in the cheap hotels of Paris with their toilet floors all cracked linoleum and scuttling beetles, the woman at the reception desk grinning so we couldn't not stare at the gap where her front teeth had been and telling us, yes I know, I know, one bed is better for you girls, also it does not cost so much and that is also a good thing, yes? We had looked young enough to get in for nothing at the Louvre and to pay only half price on the tube when we got back to London, even though in reality we were nearer twenty. In guilt-stricken love with each other for just over a year by then, a year of pure fumbling and ecstasy; I don't use the word lightly, we knew all about purity. We were high and pure as Michael Jackson's child self singing *I'll Be There*, and we knew about things like loneliness and longing, and how to hide them, how to hide our sadnesses and kindnesses. We believed in the superiority of feeling, and we believed there had to be some superiority in everything we felt since we felt it so strongly in the face of such taken-for-granted shame. I can still see our heads together, our eyes and our mouths, intent and pretty and serious as stoats, as we thought things as innocent and perilous as, for instance, that suicide must be a good thing, at the very least a truly romantic thing, something all truly romantic people would do, since people so clearly felt so much when they did it.

You know what I think? Jackie said as we watched the woman in the headscarf cross the square away from us. I think that poor woman is a very lonely person.

I didn't want to be outdone on the superior understanding of feeling. Yes, I said, yes, and a very sad person too.

We nodded sagely. The bus drew up. We loaded our rucksacks on, and the bus circled Nelson's Column, and we saw from the bus window the same woman with the headscarf leaning out of the window of her car, and behind her in the car there was a man with a thick black beard. This man was so huge, so looming, he took up nearly all the back seat. She glared up at us out of the window, and as the bus pulled away we saw the man getting out of the back of the car and running round to the driver's seat.

They were there behind the bus all the way through the city and then all the way along the motorway. We watched them out of the back window; we saw their faces below us every few yards, distorted under light and glass when we passed under the streetlamps. After three quarters of an hour we couldn't be sure if they were still coming; they weren't directly behind the bus any more. When the bus stopped to let us off in the dark outskirts of the village where my sister lived, Jackie stood at the wheel and, near breathless with fear, told the bus driver about the people following us.

So? the driver said. He shrugged his shoulders. The bus door hissed shut and left us on the verge.

We abandoned the rucksacks, left them lying. We stumbled three hundred yards along a main road so unlit that I remember the grass of the verge as black. We found the passageway to my sister's street, and when we got to her house we hammered on the door and stammered it all out on the doorstep about the woman and the man. My sister's husband phoned the police while we drank tea and ate toast and sat dazed and safe in front of their television watching *What The Papers Say*, but I could tell from the tone of his voice, embarrassed and explanatory in the hall, that he thought we were overreacting, or maybe even making it up.

So that's the first part of the story. I put my hand into the water below the foam and feel for the cutlery, try not to lift out sharp knives by their blades, and even now it makes me shake my head a little, like I would if I woke up and opened my eyes and found I couldn't focus properly; even now after all this time it terrifies me, what might have happened to us if we'd been good enough or docile or hopeless enough to have gone with that woman, when she asked, to her nice flat above Miss Selfridge.

You see, this is what I mean. I believed, and somewhere in my head I still believe, that this flat existed. Of course there wasn't a flat there at all, or if there was, it certainly wasn't hers. But all the horrors, all the things I don't want to imagine, still take place in that muffled flat, above the lit-up window displays and the darkened shop floor, the rows and rows of clothes, the silent accessories of the year 1979 and the late-evening traffic roaring past at random on the street outside.

The other thing is, my father is here visiting. I forgot to tell you. He's why I began thinking about all this. Here, he said to me earlier when we were having our lunch at the art gallery, do you remember that time you and your other friend, what's her name, were at that bus stop and that woman tried to get you into her car?

He's asleep through the front. He just turned up. I don't know how long he's staying this time. This morning I was reading a book and he arrived at the front

door. Never mind that, he said. Come on. Let's go out.
I'll take you out for your lunch. Where's your friend?
Out? Never mind. Let's go.

You wouldn't have caught him dead in an art gallery
when I was a child. Then after we'd been a few times
I realized that he wants to go there specifically so he
can say things like: What's that then? what's it called?
A Woman's Face? well it doesn't look like a woman's face
to me, it looks like a dog's dinner, unless she's really
ugly in which case she should get surgery, you know,
plastic surgery, *A Woman's Face*, is that her nose? is it?
God help her, I could do better than that and I can't
even paint, she'd have been better off with me painting
her. And what's that? what's the point of that? *Boulder
In Room*. A boulder in a room? a picture of a boulder
in a room? eh? that painter's got his sizes all wrong, his
perspective, how would that size of boulder have got
into that room? that boulder would never have, it's too
big, the room's too small, he'd never get it through the
door, you'd have had to build the bloody house round
the boulder to get a boulder that big into the room.

I used to explain, laboriously and painedly, about
cubism and surrealism and modernism and seeing
things from different perspectives. Then I realized I was
being patronizing and irrelevant, and that he wasn't
listening anyway. It's much better now when we go.
This morning we had a really nice time. We walked
round all the rooms so he could say the things and I
could nod and listen, and after that we went to the art
gallery cafeteria.

I don't know if I've ever told you this story about my

father before. When I was about nine, one summer evening I was out playing by myself, kicking around in the cinders behind the garages, and I saw a man. He was sitting in the empty square of space and rubble where a garage had been, and holding his hand down low he said, can you see? Yes, I can see, I said. I thought the man must be stupid. I wasn't blind. Then I saw that what he was holding, what he wanted me to look at, was his penis. I looked at it for a while like I was supposed to, then I waved my hand at him to say good-bye and strolled back to our garden with my hands in my pockets, rather pleased with myself, a little cocky you might say, about what I'd seen. My father was cleaning our car outside our garage. I told him about the man. Dad, guess what? I said.

I had never seen him be so lithe, move so fast. He threw down the sponge; it splashed into the bucket and sent the water slopping out over the ground. A moment later, with me falling further behind him in the mob of children drawn by the noise of something happening, there he was, my father, several strides ahead of the group of other fathers he'd gathered from the houses, and all of them racing across the field after a man who was right at the other side of it. When they reached him my father was the first there and the first to punch him down. I wasn't sure if it was the same man, but it didn't matter; all the fathers stood in a ring round him until the police came to take him back to the mental hospital, which was only half a mile away across the canal and was where he was an in-patient, the man they'd beaten. My father was a local hero for weeks after that, for months. People from the street where we lived then would probably still remember the night; it had an air of celebration, like Bonfire Night, or like the night when John Munro's father took his lawnmower and in a stroke of genius mowed a football-pitch-sized square for the first time into the long grass of that field.

I pile the bowls and cups up on each other, a bit unsafe. (Don't you feel bad about that man who got beaten up? you say behind me. Quiet, I say, I'm thinking.) These days my father can fall asleep just about anywhere with the blank ease of, say, a kitten or a puppy; I look around and he's gone again, his head down, his chin on his chest and his breathing heavy and regular. He's fallen asleep through there with the television up quite loud, and I can still hear him sighing out a rhythm over a relentlessly sincere speech of Clinton's. When I went through to collect his cup he was sleeping through footage of dead Iraqi people, a mother and a child lying poisoned where they fell in their village street, their faces bloated. I switched it off. He opened his eyes. Put it back on, he said, I'm watching the news. I switched it back on. There was a graph on the screen showing Clinton's soaring popularity, and a shot of a film star saying, we don't care how much tail he chases so long as he does his job, and my father sighed, closed his eyes and went back to sleep.

(But is it connected? I'm a bit lost, are they connected, the story about your father and the story about the woman with the headscarf? you say behind me. You throw your applecore at the bin with perfect aim; in it goes. Yes, but wait, in a minute, I say. Bear with me.)

I'm thinking how my father fell asleep at the art gallery too, after lunch, sitting on a cushioned stool. For a while I stood on the other side of the room and watched him sleeping. Lately he's grown a beard, for what I think is the first time in his life. He looks like a different man, like a salty old seadog, like Sean Connery. He told me proudly earlier about a woman flirting with him in the supermarket. I'm not surprised; he looks better now – is better-looking, is in better shape – than he was ten years ago when his business was folding. He looks a lot better than he did when he was in his mid-fifties even, that much younger than he is now, the age he would have been when Jackie and I arrived back from London full of our story, and full of lies about how we'd slept, how we'd only had one room but there'd been two beds, or how there'd only been one bed so one of us had slept on the floor. But my father and mother were distraught, hardly listened to us; so strained-looking that for the first time in my life I realized they would break; and this was all because someone had sent an unpleasant, unsigned letter to the local tax office about how my father's business was far too booming.

(Aha, you say.) But now I'm thinking of my father's shop, which sold lightbulbs made to look like candles, with pretend plastic wax dripping down their sides and bulbs whose elements flickered like flames. There were dusty stacks of batteries and plugs, and cables of all widths rolled in great reels on steel poles on the wall; there were kettles and irons and mini-fans and hairdryers, there were drawers of parts and drawers of fuses, drawers filled with anonymous bits of plastic and rubber that could make things work. Behind the counter there were two loose wires, live, for testing lightbulbs; he used to tease me, here, touch these, go on, and sometimes I would, just to get the queasy feeling all over again and to see if it really felt as horrible as I remembered. Propped on the back wall behind and above him was an old piece of cardboard from the nineteen fifties when the shop first opened. On it a dapper-suited man was demonstrating a lamp to an ecstatic woman with the words The Theme Is Power radiating like a rainbow over their heads, and over the head of my serving father, in a lit-up exclamatory arc.

His shop was next door to the Joke Shop, which had black-face soap, electric buzzers for shaking hands, fake dog's dirt and bluebottles and nails-through-the-finger, brandy glasses with the brandy sealed inside the glass so the drinker would be fooled, and special bird-call whistles which my father, whose laugh rang down the streets and round the shops from a great distance away, showed me how to use; how to tuck metal and leather into the roof of your mouth, moisten properly with your tongue, and then you could imitate any bird you heard. It sold X-ray specs, which my mother confiscated from me when she saw the sharp nail-points holding them together next to where the open eye would be.

You see, I tell you. My mother was still alive, and pretty well, when Jackie and I got back with our bus-stop story; but it was the beginning of her worrying herself awake every night wondering which acquaintance, which friend, which familiar face had sent the letter; maybe someone who'd been round for a cup of tea and had sat smiling at her in that very armchair, had complimented her on her kitchen full of shiny electrical things and their house it had taken them nearly forty years to own. It was a terrible time. A man who worked in the tax office, a neighbour, an old friend, came round; he sat on the couch and hung his head. His aftershave was apologetic. He said, usually we get these crank notes, and usually they go straight in the bucket, I'm so sorry, I didn't see it otherwise it would've. My mother patted his hand. My father gave him a whisky, patted him on the back.

(Then what happened? you ask.)

She wasted, became ill. He aged twenty years in one month. He worked with the inspector who came to take his business apart; she was young, a woman in her late twenties, and she found an accountant's old mistake in his books, charged him for that, and when she was finished she shook his hand and said she'd enjoyed her time with him and that enjoyment was a rare thing in her job. Then that was it, over. But my mother sat on a low stool in her kitchen, drinking tea on her own and staring at the food mixer, at nothing, knowing for a fact that someone had wanted to hurt her.

I turn round. You're not there. I knew that. There's no one here, just me, and my father breathing next door.

So I wipe down the table. I wipe the crumbs on to the floor instead of into my hand like I should, and my mother laughs down at me. Now that she's safe in heaven dead she tends to laugh at all the slatternly things I do, all the things that would have enraged her when she was alive. I leave a sheet on the line for two days and two nights, regardless of rain and the judgements of neighbours, and she laughs delightedly. I blow my nose on my clothes and she laughs and laughs, claps her hands. I try sewing anything, anything at all, and she roars with laughter in my ear like it's the funniest thing she's ever seen.

My mother, all her illness gone; holding the soles of her feet and rocking with laughter up there above us. When I was about thirteen, back when I felt scared and guilty all the time, I asked her once if there wasn't anything she'd done in her life that she still felt bad about. She was getting ready to go out to work. Her hand paused by her mouth holding the lipstick, and her face went thoughtful. Yes, she said suddenly, lots of things, and she laughed, then her face fell, she looked crushed, she sat down on the side of the bed. Yes, there was the time someone stole my new shoes and it was my fault, and my mother, your granny, I'd never seen her so angry. We were poor. I've told you before, though you can't imagine what that means. We were poor but your granny always made sure we had shoes, it was a thing of decency for her. So there was one year we got our new shoes for going back to school, but my best friend was barefoot and I wanted to be too. I didn't want to be any different. So I took my new shoes off and I hid them in the grass outside the school, and I was barefoot all day. But when I came out they were gone, someone had taken them. It was terrible. It was the end of the world. I had to go home to my mother with no shoes.

She sat on the bed with the wardrobe door open

opposite her, and she waved her hand over all the shoes, hundreds of shoes hardly scuffed, piled several-thick inside each other and on top of each other on the wardrobe floor. Look at that now, she said. Then she lifted the hairspray tin and shook it. This'll chase you, she said. Off you go you monkey, I'm going to be late because of you, or if you're staying, cover your eyes and take a deep breath, I'm going to spray.

(I still don't really get the connection, you say.) Well, no. Okay. Actually you don't say anything, you're not home yet. But you'll be home soon, so I imagine your key in the door, you kicking off your shoes and hanging your jacket in the hall, and coming through, stealing up behind me and kissing the back of my neck. Your face will be cold, and when I turn to kiss you back, your nose will be cold and you'll taste of outside. You'll say, you're doing the dishes, what's happened, has the world changed? is someone here? is your father here? your father must be here. You'll point to the drying crockery. You'll stand back to admire its pile-up, like people admiring art. Brilliant, you'll say. Pure sculpture.

You always say something like that.

And then it's later, it's late, it's nearly midnight now, and you're home. You came home half an hour after I finished the dishes. Now my father is in bed in the spare room. I can hear him snoring all the way through two walls. It's disturbing, as usual. It's too familiar.

I'm lying in bed. You're tired; you're not saying much. You didn't say much at supper. I think you might be in a bad mood. You undress, folding your clothes as you take them off.

I'm a little worried for my father. It can be cold in the spare room; I should have given him a hot water bottle. I think of his shop, dark and gone. The last time I passed it, it had become a clan heraldry shop, its windows full of little shields; a bored-looking man sat behind the counter and there were no customers. I think of the art gallery today, and the picture we saw with the massive rock in the room and the door blocked behind it. My head full of dark thoughts, I think of Jackie again, of how finally we betrayed each other, fell out of love, in love with others; we couldn't not.

I stop thinking about it all. It's too sore.

Outside someone goes past, a drunk angry man, and it sounds like he's hitting the cars parked along the road with a stick or his fist. He's shouting. I'm doing your fucking cars, he shouts. You better come out and get me. None of yous will. You're all fucking cowards. I'm going to do all your fucking cars.

His voice fades as he moves down the road. You get into bed. You switch the bedside light out, and we're in the dark. You sigh.

Listen, I say, and I want to tell you the whole story, but it rolls around dangerously in my head. So I say,

What if there was a great big boulder in the room, and you've no idea how it got in, it's so much bigger than the door.

What? you say. You turn beside me, speaking into my back.

A boulder. It's nearly as big as the room, I say. And it's slowly coming towards you –

Towards me? you say.

Towards us, I say, and it's crushing all the things in the room.

It'd better not, you say. We haven't paid this bed off yet, I'm not having it destroyed by a stupid, what is it, boulder?

But listen. What if there was a great big stone in the room, I say, big enough to almost be up to the ceiling, and as wide as from there to there.

A stone, you say sleepily. As big as the room. Coming towards us. Where's my chisel? get me a chisel, find something we can use as a hammer. You'd pay a fortune for that much rock at a stonemason's.

Under the covers you take my hand and turn it around, put your fingers through mine, interlocked, and you fall asleep like that, holding my hand.

That's all it takes. One glance, one sidelong blow from you, and a rock as big as a room explodes into little bits of gravel. I pick around in the shards of it, remember someone I saw today in the art gallery, a stranger, a man who sat down next to my sleeping father with such care, trying not to wake him. I remember my father like he was way back then, showing me the inside of a plug and which colour went where; and I think of my father now, flirting with a woman in a supermarket, playfully circling each other in the checkout queue. I make the woman very good-looking, to please him, and a little like my mother, to please us both. I remember the man I saw all those years ago in the space where the garage had been, cradling his genitals like he was holding a creature, something new-born, furless; and the fathers, stupid with protection, hurling themselves along the backs of the houses; and my mother telling me to shield my eyes so the hairspray chemicals wouldn't get in them. And then I think back to Jackie and me in London waiting at that bus stop, two teenage girls in a random city, good enough to believe the lies that a stranger told, even caring in the first place that a stranger might be sad.

You're next to me asleep with my hand still in yours, my father is snoring along the hall, and I'm not long from sleep myself. I lie in our unpaid bed and trust you, carelessly, precariously, with my whole heart. That's the story finished, that's all there is to it. One last time though, before I lock the door on it for the night, turn the sign from Open to Closed, I picture Jackie, wherever she is, wherever she might be in the world.

I imagine she's holding such a hand. I imagine her safe and sound.

The book club

The girl who went missing was the same age as I was. Her school photograph was in the papers and on the Scottish news on television, which I found very exciting at the time since nothing about where we lived was ever on television, not even Scottish television. I was ten. I spent the long light nights that summer playing by myself in and out of the greenhouse my father was putting up in our back garden. It had no plants or glass in it yet, just the concrete floor, the frame of its sides and roof and the new door stiff in its runners. I could put my arm through glass that wasn't there and imagine it passing through solid wall, like in The Bionic Woman. I could lean out of the top half of the door like it was a stable door, or crouch down under the metal bar across its middle and walk through the bottom half of it without opening it.

I heard my father over the fence talking to someone by the garages. He called me out of our garden. She loves books, he was saying to the man. Here, he said to me, this man says he'll let you choose any book you like out of his van, then when you've read it you can give it back to him and get another one.

The man's name was Stephen; he sold books round the Highlands and Islands. The inside of his van was all books. It had folding steps at the back doors; it was all right to go in because my father had said it was. It wasn't a library, they weren't for borrowing, they were for selling. They had titles like Papillon and Shogun. I chose one about someone looking for someone, with the actress I now know to be Diane Keaton on the cover smiling and smoking a cigarette; I chose it because she was pretty.

If you're careful with it, the man from the van said, I'll be able to sell it on.

He showed me how to hold it and bend it gently so the spine wouldn't crease and so I wouldn't smear the page-edge with dirty hands. I read it in bed. It was about sex, then somebody killed her. Each night I held the book like he'd shown me because of the person who would be reading it after me, maybe someone who lived out on one of the islands. Someone up there would buy it from the van and would have it in their house and I had to make sure they would never know I had read it before them. There was a girl from the Outer Hebrides at my school. She spoke like her words had extra sounds to them, fussy-edged like the lace things my mother stuck with long pins on to the backs and arms of the new three-piece suite in the front room.

My mother, eyeing me blank and steady over the breakfast plates.

Iona, you're looking a bit pale, she said. Come here.

She felt my head. I had been awake long after everybody else, reading and re-reading the bits about sex and the part at the end where the man did it, holding the book as hardly open as possible with my head at an angle to try to make out the words at the hidden inside ends of the lines.

I was up late reading, I said.

She pushed the butter into her toast, hard and spare with the knife. Neither of my parents read books. If you worked you had no time for it. My mother especially had no time for it, she saw no point in it, which is why it's still surprising to me that one of the very few things I have of hers now, ten years after her death, is a book. Rip Van Winkle and other stories by Washington Irving. She gave it to me one afternoon when I was in my twenties, home from college for the summer; you can have this, she said. God knows where she'd kept it, I'd never seen it before and I knew every book in the house. It was a school book. It has her maiden name and the name of her school written in neat handwriting inside a printed shield saying This Book Belongs To, and her name scrawled in blotted blue capitals all along the page edge in messy different-sized letters. Its date of publication is 1938, the year her father died and she had to leave school. She was fourteen. Now I have the book, her grey leather driving gloves and her wedding ring.

I am thinking about all this between the airport and home, in a black cab crossing the South-East of England. The driver is keen to talk to me, I can sense it. I take a book out of my bag and hold it ready, though I know if I do actually try to read it I will get motion sickness. It's a book that was on a lot of shortlists last year. It's written by a man and the trick of it is that it's written as if a woman were writing it. Everybody says it's good. I turn it over in my hand. It smells of my father's tomatoes. I hold it to my nose and fan its pages. My bag is full of tomatoes, some near-ripe, some still green. I am supposed to put them on my windowsill when I get home.

The driver half turns towards me. I open the book in the middle. I glance at it, then out of the window. The grass on the road verges is high again, the fields the gold colour they go at this time of year. I press a button by my armrest and the glass to my right slides down. Summer air comes in. The summers go round and round, they seem not to get any older at all, they seem smooth, repetitive, summer back again, but really they date as hopelessly as if you put an old 45 on a turntable, or maybe took an old 45 off a turntable and skimmed it into a canal on a still day like today then stood staring at the surface where there's nothing to say anything ever skimmed across it or sank below it or happened at all.

Now the driver is asking me something. Excuse me, he is saying from behind his divide. Where do you want?

His voice sounds amplified but far away. I've already told him where we're meant to be going. What if we're going the wrong way? I don't have that much cash on me and already the animated circle on his meter which lights a new piece of itself every three or four seconds and means ten pence each time the circle completes itself has completed itself an alarming number of times and we're only just on the outskirts of Luton.

I tell him the name of the town again.

No, but where? he says.

Near the centre, I'll tell you when we get there, I shout at the divide.

But where exactly? he says. The street you live in. How is it spelled?

You won't know it, I shout. It's very small.

You don't need to speak so loud, he says. I can hear you.

Without taking his eyes off the road he points to a sign above the back of his head. When the light is on, the sign says, you may speak to your driver.

Oh, right, I shout. Then I speak more normally. The street I live in is very small, I say, but when we get there I'll tell you which way to go.

No, he says. Because look.

He has a screen stuck to his dashboard about the size of a paperback. He flips its insides down and open. He punches some buttons.

I just told it the city we're going to, he says.

A voice comes out of the screen, the voice of a middle-class English lady. She says: *at the next roundabout, continue straight ahead.* Words appear on the screen at the same time saying the same thing.

We come to a roundabout. We continue straight ahead.

So where do you live exactly? the driver says.

He enters the name of my street into his machine. Several maps flash up. That's where you live, isn't it? is that where you live? he is saying. There? He swivels his head from me to the road ahead then back to me then to the road again. The cab swerves as he turns. I slide about on the seat.

Yes, I say.

See? he says. It's good, isn't it? It can tell you about

anywhere. Anywhere you ask it. Anywhere at all. It sends a signal to the satellite and the satellite sends a signal back.

He points at a small dark box fitted on to the other side of his cab.

And you can have the voice on to tell you, or just the words on here if you don't want to listen to the voice, or both, if you want both, or neither, if you don't want a voice or the information, he says.

He switches the voice on and off to show me. He turns its volume up and down. He is a lot younger than me. It's a new cab. Everything metal about it is reflecting light and its grey insides are new. It says on a sticker by my hand on the door the words Made In Coventry With Pride.

It cost eighteen hundred, he says, and that's not all it does. It tells you, look, it tells you all these things.

At the next roundabout, the lady's voice says, *continue straight ahead*.

He presses a series of buttons one after another.

It tells me the fastest route, he says. And the route that is quietest. It tells me exactly how many miles till I have to turn left or right. It tells me about roadworks. It tells me how many miles it is to your house, not just to the city but right to your house. And look, it can tell me the route that saves me petrol, and when we get to town it will tell me exactly which way to go to get to your house and exactly how many yards before I have to turn left or right to get there. See that roadsign? What does it say?

Bedford 15 miles, I say.

Look on here, look, what does it say?

Bedford 15 miles, I say.

Exactly, he says. Exactly. So if we wanted to go to Bedford, we would know for certain without needing a roadsign that it's only fifteen miles away. Did you ever travel in a cab like this before?

No, I say, this is my first.

I wonder to myself if it is an elaborate chat-up technique. Do you want to go to Bedford. He tells me that soon all cabs and probably all cars will have navigation systems like his.

My name is Wasim, he says. I'll give you my mobile number and whenever you need a cab from Luton you can call me and I'll always fetch you from the airport.

What? he says when I tell him my name. How is it spelled?

He tries to make sense of it.

It sounds like three words, not one, he says.

It's the name of an island, I say. It's a place. You could type it into your machine and find me on it.

Ha ha, he says. But where are you from, if it is okay to ask?

I point to the screen. You know exactly, I say.

Ah, he says. No, before that. You're from somewhere else. I can tell by the way you speak.

At the next junction, the middle-class lady's voice says, *turn left*.

He tells me he has a cousin who works in Glasgow. I tell him Glasgow's not really near where I'm from.

I visited, he says. It rained.

He lifts both hands off the wheel in a shrug which

takes in the whole country round us, deep in its afternoon sun.

I nod and smile. I sit back.

Are you too hot? Do you need air-conditioning? Tell
me if you need anything, he says.

I'm fine, I say. Thank you.

If you want to go to sleep, go ahead, he says. I'll
wake you when you're near home.

He flicks a switch on the dashboard. The little red
light above his head goes out.

Her name was Carolyn Fergusson, she lived down
the Ferry, it was before the new bridge and I can
remember the posters stuck on the shop windows with
her school photograph on them, she looked sad. They
found her in her uncle's house up in Kinmylies hidden
all over the place in supermarket bags in the cupboards,
I remember a friend of my parents coming round to
the house and telling them; he knew because he worked
at the police labs, and that the smell when they went
in was really terrible even though the summer hadn't
been nearly as hot as the one the year before; they were
in the kitchen talking about it and I was listening
through the door and when they heard me there my
mother shouted at me to go out to the back garden and
bring the washing in. That summer I Feel Love by
Donna Summer was number one for weeks and after
it the Brotherhood of Man. Running away together,
running away for ever, Angelo. Whenever I hear those
songs now I think of then. We weren't supposed to leave
our gardens; we were supposed to stay where our
parents could see us at all times. The following summer

we could go where we liked again and I can't remember what was number one.

Next to the tomatoes in the bag is the lump of defrosting soup in its Tupperware container; he wrapped it in newspaper to keep it cool. He is refusing to take any of the pills his doctor told him to take. He was proud about it. You're being stupid, I said. Rubbish, he said, they do you more harm than good. He took me out into his garden and pointed at some huge concrete slabs by the greenhouse and said, as soon as you've gone I'm going to take those seven slabs up and put them back down on the other side of the garden and then I can swing the caravan round on to them, and then there's a fridge-freezer in the garage I'm going to move into the house later today if I can get it through the door. You are joking, aren't you, I said. But he's a bit deaf in one ear and he was looking away from me with the wrong ear turned towards me, he didn't answer.

I feel the cab turn left. The soup is wrapped in newspaper covered with the story of the missing schoolgirls, which is why, I suppose, I'm even thinking of Carolyn Fergusson. It's pushed the build-up of war on to the second and third and international pages. It's always in the summer they go missing, as if it's the right season for it, as if the people who take them have been waiting, like farmers or fruit pickers or tabloid editors, for the right weather to kick in for it. When I was about twelve and got home late one summer night, when they'd been calling me and calling me all round the neighbourhood to come in and I hadn't heard, they were so angry that they threw me round the kitchen, my father grabbing one arm as my mother let go of the other. I bounced off the units. I was bruised all over. She was particularly good at being furious, slamming the prongs of her fork into a piece of potato at the dinner table, warningly looking away from me and saying nothing, and because the saying nothing was so much worse than the saying something I remember her saying:

I swear Iona, in a minute it'll be the back of my hand.

You'll be the death of me, girl.

You'll be sorry when I'm gone.

Then I remember something I haven't thought about for years. She was standing at the table flicking through a magazine and she held the magazine up and looked at me across the room. It was summer. I was sitting on the couch watching anything on TV. I was seventeen and sullen. She flapped the magazine in the air.

I think we should join this, she said.

It would be something about sewing or Catholicism or being more like a girl was supposed to be. I watched the TV as if something very important was on.

For only a penny each, she said, if you send to these people, you can get four books. A penny each. There are all these books you can choose from on this page. All you have to do is buy their Book of the Month. And then what they do, after that, they send you their Book of the Month every month for a year and you don't have to buy it if you don't want it. They have all these things you can choose from for a penny. The Collected Works of William Shakespeare. That would be a useful book for you to have.

What? I said, because I had been fighting for nearly a year to be allowed to do English at university, not Law or Languages but something that meant I would never have a proper job. I can see myself now coming across the room, my eyes wide, my face like a child's, or like someone whose hopelessly foreign language has suddenly been understood, and my mother pleased with herself, holding out the open page to me.

We ordered the Shakespeare collection and a dictionary and a thesaurus and a book of quotations. Four weeks later they came all together in a box through the post and with them was the hardback Book Club Book of the Month which was called Princess Anne and her Horses and was full of colour photographs of Princess Anne and horses. My mother laughed and laughed. Then she saw the price of the book.

The following month the Book of the Month was a book about royal palaces. The month after that it was about the life of an English Edwardian lady. The month after that it was about the history of fox-hunting. They came every month, about gardens and the stately homes of members of royalty, always glossy with colour plates, expensive unwieldy hardbacks and my mother, who kept forgetting to send them back before the crucial eight days' return time, kept having to pay for them. They were stacked in the back room on the floor under the coffee table and there were more each time I came home at the end of a term.

I am wondering where all those useless books ended up, where they are now, whether they are still piled up unread somewhere in my father's house, when I hear the taxi driver speak. I open my eyes. The red light above his head is lit.

See how close we are, he says.

At the back of his voice the middle-class lady's voice is telling him to turn left in twenty yards.

Nearly home, he says.

Nearly home, I say.

He edges his cab between the cars parked on either side of the narrow roads before my own narrow road. He drives well.

You laughed in your sleep, he says. It must have been a good sleep.

He pulls up outside my house. It isn't as much on the meter as I thought it'd be. It is exactly the amount he told me it would be. I get the money out and count it and try to scrape together a good enough tip and I want to ask him, who called you Wasim? was it your mother or your father? is it after someone? does it mean something? what does it mean? I want to say, are you married? have you any children? are your parents still living? are they old enough to be supposed to be taking medication for anything and are they refusing to? did you grow up in Luton? what was it like to? what's it like there since Vauxhall closed and so many people lost their jobs? can we not just drive somewhere else, choose a place at random? could we go somewhere and not know where we're going till we got there? could we leave the navigation system off and just see where we ended up?

I get out of the cab and give him the money.

Thank you, I say.

Your book, he says. Don't forget.

I reach back in and pick it up off the seat.

He is looking at his watch now. Look, he says. We made good time. We took good roads. We were lucky.

He writes his number on the back of a receipt and I tell him I'll call him next time I need to come home. He drives up to the end of the road and round the corner, out of sight. I find my keys, unlock my front door, go in and close it behind me.

Extract from The Accidental

I was born in the year of the supersonic, the era of the multistorey multivitamin multitonic, the highrise time of men with the technology and women who could be bionic, when jump-jets were Harrier, when QE2 was Cunard, when thirty-eight feet tall the Princess Margaret stood stately in her hoverpad, the année érotique was only thirty aircushioned minutes away and everything went at twice the speed of sound. I opened my eyes. It was all in colour. It didn't look like Kansas any more. The students were on the barricades, the mode was maxi, the Beatles were transcendental, they opened a shop. It was Britain. It was great. My mother was a nun who could no longer stand the convent. She married my father, the captain; he was very strict. She taught us all to sing and made us new clothes out of curtains. We ran across the bridges and jumped up and down the steps. We climbed the trees and fell out of the boat into the lake. We came first in the singing contest and narrowly escaped the Nazis.

I was formed and made in the Saigon days, the Rhodesian days, the days of the rivers of blood. DISEMBOWEL ENOCH POWELL. Apollo 7 splashdowned. Tunbridge Wells was flooded. A crowd flowed over London Bridge, and thirty-six Americans made bids to buy it. They shot the king in Memphis, which delayed the Academy Awards telecast for two whole days. He had a dream, he held these truths to be self-evident, that all men were created equal and would one day sit down together at the table of brotherhood. They shot the other brother at the Ambassador Hotel. RIGHTEOUS BROS it said in lights, above the hotel car park. Meanwhile my father was the matchmaker and my mother could fly using only her umbrella. When I was a child I ran the Grand National on my horse. They didn't know I was a girl until I fainted and they unbuttoned my jockey shirt. But anything was possible. We had a flying floating car. We stopped the rail disaster by waving our petticoats at the train; my father was innocent in prison, my mother made ends meet. I sold flowers in Covent Garden. A posh geezer taught me how to speak proper and took me to the races, designed by Cecil Beaton, though they dubbed my voice in the end because the singing wasn't good enough.

But my father was Alfie, my mother was Isadora. I was unnaturally psychic in my teens, I made a boy fall off his bike and I burned down a whole school. My mother was crazy; she was in love with God. There I was at the altar about to marry someone else when my boyfriend hammered on the church glass at the back and we eloped together on a bus. My mother was furious. She'd slept with him too. The devil got me pregnant and a satanic sect made me go through with it. Then I fell in with a couple of outlaws and did me some talking to the sun. I said I didn't like the way he got things done. I had sex in the back of the old closing cinema. I used butter in Paris. I had a farm in Africa. I took off my clothes in the window of an apartment building and distracted the two police inspectors from watching for the madman on the roof who was trying to shoot the priest. I fell for an Italian. It was his moves on the dancefloor that did it. I knew what love meant. It meant never having to say you're sorry. It meant the man who drove the taxi would kill the presidential candidate, or the pimp. It was soft as an easy chair. It happened so fast. I had my legs bitten off by the shark. I stabbed the kidnapper, but so did everybody else, it wasn't just me, on the Orient Express.

My father was Terence and my mother was Julie. (Stamp. Christie.) I was born and bred by the hills (alive) and the animals (talked to). I considered myself well in, part of the furniture. There wasn't a lot to spare. Who cared? I put on a show, right here in the barn; I was born singing the song at the top of my just-formed lungs. Inchworm. Inchworm. Measuring the marigolds. Seems to me you'd stop and see how beautiful they are. I rose inch by inch with the international rise of the nose of Streisand, the zee of Liza. What good was sitting alone in my room? When things went decimal I was ready for it.

I was born in a time of light, speed, celluloid. Downstairs was smoking. The balcony was non. It cost more money to sit in the balcony.

The kinematograph. The eidoloscope. The galloping tintypes. The silver screen. The flicks. The pictures. Up rose the smoke. Misty watercolour memories.

But it's all in the game and the way you play it, and you've got to play the game, you know.

I was born free, I've had the time of my life and for all we know I'm going to live for ever.

Trachtenbauer

A tiny little schoolboy with the name of Trachtenbauer was at my door when I opened it.

I say tiny little and that's literally what I mean. He was about eight inches tall, the size of a sizeable penis, the average height of a cat, which meant that when the doorbell rang while I was pouring my cornflakes into the bowl and I went through to the hall thinking it would be the postman and opened the door and looked out, it was as if there was no one there at all, and it was only as I was about to close it that I heard the squeaking of a small voice at shin level.

Hello! he squeaked. I am Trachtenbauer.

I looked down.

Grey cap, little red shield on the front; grey, blue and red striped blazer, little red shield on the top pocket; white shirt, top button buttoned at the collar; tight knotted blue-and-red striped school tie tucked into grey pullover; grey shorts; grey kneesocks; perfectly-tailored diminutive leather brogues as if created, designed and sewn by tiny hands in the leathery sweatshop of an imagination like Enid Blyton's.

How did you reach the doorbell? I said.

Maths, of course, he squeaked. I calculated the square-metred area of your front doorstep and the closest angle of elevation from which to launch a small missile i.e. a pebble from your driveway. I am top at maths. I am naturally brilliant at many things and it helps that most of my talents have been nurtured by excellent schooling and supremely good parenting. And I'm here today to tell you that all of these things are available to everybody in this country, rich or poor, who works hard and plays fair, and that we're jolly lucky to be living at such a lucky and civilized time, don't you agree?

Eh, I suppose so, I said.

The tiny little schoolboy glowed at my feet as if he'd just won a debating trophy.

You may at this still quite early stage in the story be feeling cheated and annoyed, if you, like me, like your short stories to be about real things in the real world. You may be feeling frustrated, too, if what you like in fiction is the kind of story where what people have for breakfast and how they spoon it from bowl to mouth or scrape whatever they take on their toast on to their toast, reveals not just their characters but their whole lives held there in one perfectly pitched moment; how their slightest movements round the wood or Formica tables in their kitchens, how they brush their teeth before they leave for work in the mornings, reveals the emotional gains and losses of their lives. I understand. Here's some contemporary verisimilitude. A woman is standing blindfolded in a communal cell in Abu Ghraib and her dead brother's body is brought and dumped at her feet. She doesn't know for sure if it's her brother, but that's what they shouted in English when they dumped him: here's your brother. Her sister is standing in the same cell. She is also blindfolded. The woman crouches down, puts her tied hands down and feels a slick of something warm on the body. Is it blood? She doesn't know. She can't see. She raises her hands to her nose. It smells like blood. She stands up again. It's difficult to stand up when you're blindfolded and your hands are tied. She senses her sister kneeling down now. She says to her sister: is he breathing? Her sister answers, but only after several minutes.

No.

So, back here in the UK, I opened my door and at my feet was an eight-inch-high perfect representation of a public schoolboy.

Not representation, he squeaked. I'm not a representation. I'm the real thing.

What did you say your name was? I said.

Trachtenbauer, he said. Trachtenbauer. Trachtenbauer. Trachtenbauer. It's an old English family name.

It sounds a bit German to me, I said.

Yes, he said. To the uninitiated ear it would sound German. But the original Trachtenbauers are listed in the Domesday Book. I am not lying. I never lie. I cannot tell a lie. I'd never lie to you. I do however have fun in my advanced German class with the many hilarious random things my name could be translated to mean, were it by any stretch of the imagination a name that wasn't wholly English. For example. Farmer of costumes. Costumed cage. Endeavouring farmer. Cage of striving. Dressed-up cage. Endeavouring cage. Endeavouring pawn. Dressed-up pawn.

Dressed-up porn? I said.

Pawn, he squeaked. As in chessboard, lowest ranking piece. Pawn. Pawn.

To my amazement he went completely red with anger. He was waving his minute fists in the air. He was stamping his tiny feet on my doorstep and squeaking the word pawn over and over. It really did sound like porn; well, upper-middle-class porn. I closed the front door. I'd had enough of him, frankly. I didn't want a hysterical public schoolboy, even that small a one, in my house.

To tell you the truth I didn't really want to have to be taking part in this kind of story either. It's not the kind of story I'd have chosen, myself. I'd have preferred something much more utilitarian and social. I went, when I was a schoolgirl, to one of the first Scottish comprehensives. This was, oh, years and years before nine eleven. Of course, the world's completely changed now, as we all know. Nothing can possibly be the same again. I remember, from those old gone days, the feeling of being sixteen and knowing I could say: nuclear power, no thanks. I had the leaflets. I wore the badge. My father nodded. He said, that's how change happens, girl, that's how history happens, through people like you questioning the status quo.

My father, by the way, is a brilliant man now in his eighties, who had to leave school in his early teens because his mother needed him to earn money, after his own father, who'd been gassed in the First World War, died. He worked as an electrician all his life. He and my mother put all five of us, me and my four siblings, through a tertiary education that they never even had the dream of having. Both of them were clever. Neither of them was still at school past the age of thirteen. When my father was nineteen he saw, over the side of a Royal Navy cruiser on its way to Sicily, forty American soldiers who'd been wrongly parachuted in and had landed miles out in the Mediterranean, and they were calling to each passing ship in the convoy to stop for them and pick them up. When he saw them waving in the water, trying to keep their heads above the wake, and he knew that no ship was ever going to stop for them, that was his education.

As to his children's education, I can see him sitting in his chair by the electric fire and tapping the arm of it with his finger. Because when that war was over, the good thing that came of it, he believed, was that everyone knew that the sons of the poor and the ordinary were equal to the sons of the rich, equally able to go to Eton, to Oxford, to Cambridge – maybe even if they happened to be daughters.

So when I was a schoolgirl, at the height of comprehensive education, we once spent an evening in the same building as the boys and girls of Gordonstoun, school of the royals, at a schools-night performance of Macbeth at the theatre in Inverness, which is where I grew up. It was 1978, one of the years of punk, so we had what you might call a common language. There was a lot of giving each other the finger after that performance through the bus windows in the car park of the theatre, and remembering this now makes me think of my sister Anne's trick when she was a schoolgirl ten years earlier than me, whenever her school hockey team was playing a team from a private school, of dribbling effortlessly past public schoolgirl after public schoolgirl simply by saying as she approached with the ball on her stick, Excuse me, Excuse me.

But don't go thinking that what I've been telling you is going to transform this uneasy hybrid of fantasy and reality into something resolved in the end by a bit of touching autobiographical material. Because it won't. This is a Trachtenbauer time we live in.

So I closed the front door on him and went through to the kitchen to have my breakfast, and there he was, standing in the middle of the room, enthusiastic as anything.

Hello again! he said. He was bright as a button. Actually I quite liked his enthusiasm. It would have been hard not to. It was very endearing. The Mediterranean, he said, is the inland sea separating Europe from North Africa with Asia to the east. Its surface comprises 2,966,000 square kilometres.

Thanks for that, I said. How did you get in here, again?

Simple, he said. Catflap. It is a magnet-protected catflap, as you presumably know, since you presumably installed it, but being a schoolboy I am never without a magnet.

Ah, I said. Of course.

When your magnet-protected catflap clicked open I vaulted in, in a single vault, he said. It was a particularly good vault. I also happen to be best at sport. I am really hoping with all my heart for a Great British Olympics in 2012. Incidentally, I hope you don't mind me saying so, but you are obese.

I'm not obese! I said. I'm only nine and a half stone!

Like so many of our UK contemporary public, if you only ate a lot less and didn't eat a solid diet of saturated fatty foods like for example chips or crisps, you too would be able to pass through smaller openings, he said. But the main thing is, don't worry. There's a helpline. I can give you the number for it.

He looked a little larger than his original eight inches now himself. Maybe I had mis-seen him the first time, but he looked about a foot and a half high. It was as if he was actually growing in stature now that he'd got himself into the house. He was big enough to reach and pick a knife up off the table, which he was doing now, examining it to see what it was made of. He put it down again. He nodded to himself as if confirming something. He looked all round my kitchen and nodded some more.

Cornflakes, he said approvingly and nodded.

Look, I said. I'm very busy. What is it you actually want?

I don't want anything, he said. You want me. I'm your free government initiative.

Initiative for what? I said.

For initiative, Trachtenbauer said. Congratulations. You've been selected as a test household. Soon everyone will have me, or be able to phone a freephone number and get extra copies of me, even copies in Urdu and Bengali and French and Chinese and Welsh and Arabic and Punjabi for people who happen not to speak English well enough for the English version of me.

You mean, there's more than one of you? I said.

I am unique, but soon to be made available to millions, he said.

But what if I don't want to be a test household? I said. What if I don't want you?

Don't want me? Trachtenbauer said.

He laughed as if he couldn't imagine anything more ridiculous.

The value of your property will have risen notably since I arrived, he said. You get a better mortgage with a Trachtenbauer. You can trust a Trachtenbauer.

But don't you have a first name I could call you? Trachtenbauer feels a bit, well, unwieldy, I said.

I do, but I'm afraid I'm not permitted to tell you it, he said.

Why not? I said.

Our focus groups have decided that it's better if I'm called Trachtenbauer so that there's just a small something lingering at the back of you-the-consumer's mind to remind you of the last world war. Remember? when Britain was right? when Britain was victorious? he said.

Look, I said. This is private property. I'm asking you politely to leave.

I'm afraid this boy just can't do that, mate, he squeaked. This boy's your friend. This boy's here to stay. This boy'd never run out on you. This boy stood on the burning deck whence all but he had fled.

What? I said.

The boy stood on the burning deck whence all but he had fled, he said. The flame that lit the battle's wreck shone round him o'er the dead. Yet beautiful and bright he stood, as born to rule the storm; A creature of heroic blood, a proud, though child-like form. It's a poem by Mrs Felicia Hemans, a lady writer. Would you like to hear my Gang Show song?

No, I said. I'm going upstairs. I'll be down in ten minutes. And if you're not gone from here by the time I get downstairs, I'm calling the police.

It's you they'd arrest, though, not me, Trachtenbauer said.

Why? I said. Why would anyone arrest me? I haven't done anything wrong.

Trachtenbauer shrugged. He gave me a burning look. He put his schoolbag on the floor and leaned one arm on a tiny hip-bone.

You've been warned, I said.

You've been warned, he squeaked back. They'll keep you in prison for as long as they like, too.

I couldn't believe the schoolboy cheek of it. I went upstairs into the bathroom and put toothpaste on my toothbrush and I knew as soon as I looked in the mirror and saw myself there unchanged, same as ever, that I'd simply been hallucinating. I wondered if I'd maybe been drinking the night before and had simply forgotten how drunk I'd been. I wondered if I'd ingested a drug that had made me hallucinate. Because there was no way on earth, no way in any trustworthy verisimilitude, that a small pert schoolboy a foot and a half high had got into my house.

No.

It was as ridiculous to think this as it was to imagine that anyone, never mind a tiny little schoolboy with the name of Trachtenbauer, had just told me that the police could, for instance, arrest me, an innocent person, and hold me indefinitely without charge. Nobody could do that to the law. I lived in the kind of country where, just like short stories were short stories and behaved appropriately, the law was the law and was there to protect people from this kind of thing. It was every bit as mad to imagine such a travesty as it was to conjure up a tiny little schoolboy who came preaching into my life through the catflap; as insane as it would be if I were to look out of the bathroom window now, look up into the sky and see that the sky itself was shrouded, the whole real world was tented over with an enormous blazered Trachtenbauer so huge that he hid the sky, so that not just my house, not just my street, but the whole town, maybe the whole country, was the plaything of a giant schoolboy who, when he leaned in with his huge hand, a hand as big as five good arable fields, bigger than five football pitches, and moved something from one area of his model village to another, he knocked a small copse of trees down and wrecked a busy traffic junction and tore up the foundations of three adjoining streets as he did, by mistake, because it would be impossible not to have some innocent casualties if your hands were so big and what you were dealing with was so small.

No.

I opened the bathroom window and leaned out. The world looked the same. Everything was happening as it usually did on a weekday morning. There were people walking up and down the street. There were people going back and fore in cars. There were leaves shifting in the wind on the trees and birds singing in the gardens. There were small fluffed clouds in a bright blue sky.

I brushed my teeth.

But when I came downstairs again I found the cat cowering in a corner of the hall licking a bleeding gash in her leg.

Trachtenbauer, who now seemed nearly the size of a normal ten-year-old child, was sitting crosslegged on the carpet in my front room folding the pages he was ripping out of my Penguin Classics copy of Robert Tressell's The Ragged Trousered Philanthropists into origami swans.

What are you doing to my book? I shouted.

Top at origami, he squeaked in a squeak that was a little noticeably deeper than his previous squeaks. Animal Farm next. Have you any other outdated books you won't be needing any more? Don't think much of your taste, I'm afraid. No Biggles. No Just-so stories. No Harry Potter.

Trachtenbauer, did you just hurt my cat? I said.

Your cat attacked me, he squeaked. It's a terrorist.

He brandished a pair of bloodied eyebrow tweezers in the air.

Right, I said. That's it. I'm off out. And when I come back I'll have two alsatians with me, and believe me, they won't be scared of tweezers.

I pulled on my coat. He scuttled across the room sending origami swans flying and stood between me and the front door with his arms flung out wide.

You mustn't go out without being prepared, he said.

Prepared for what? I said.

An emergency, he said. It could happen at any time. Do you know where and how to turn off the water, gas and electricity supplies?

But he was now definitely taller, about four feet tall,

and growing, and I saw for the first time that under the too-small school cap, rather than the clear face of a boy he had the strangely wizened, strangely shrunken face of a man in his late forties or early fifties.

Keep calm, he shouted. Nothing to worry about. Go in. Stay in. Tune in. Local radio will keep you informed. Whatever you do, don't panic.

He smiled as he blocked my doorway. I had to get past him. What could I do?

Excuse me, I said.

He stepped to the side without thinking. I slipped past him and out through the door into the front garden, fast as I could go down the path. When I turned back I saw him in my doorway; his buttons were bulging now across his chest, his shorts were strained at their seams and, as I watched, his stripey blazer ripped in two and hung off both his arms like ragged Union Jacks.

Trachtenbauer, I shouted from the gate. You're getting . . . so big.

He nodded, he was all enthusiasm; I saw him swelling and swelling, taller and wider; he was much bigger than me now, and now he was as high as my downstairs rooms, and now he jutted a shoulder under the doorframe of the front door and broke it, effortlessly, shattering the bricks and plaster of my house, it had taken him only a few seconds to, and when he spoke his voice broke too, it rumbled out of him like a tank.

I'm coming of age, he said.

POCKET PENGUINS

POCKET PENGUINS